Emily, Moonshine and Sister Goose

Story and Illustrations by
Susanne Lansonius

ISBN 0-88839-403-9
Copyright ©1997 Susanne Lansonius

Cataloging in Publication Data

Lansonius, Susanne.
        Emily, Moonshine and Sister Goose

        ISBN 0-88839-403-9

1. Inuit -- Juvenile fiction. I. Title.
PS8573.A5868E44 1997   jC813′.54   C97-910293-6
PZ7.L289Em 1997

Production: Andrew Jaster
Editor: Nancy Miller

Published simultaneously in Canada and the United States by

HANCOCK HOUSE PUBLISHERS LTD.
19313 Zero Avenue, Surrey, BC V4P 1M7
(604) 538-1114   Fax (604) 538-2262

HANCOCK HOUSE PUBLISHERS
1431 Harrison Avenue, Blaine, WA 98230-5005
(604) 538-1114   Fax (604) 538-2262

This story is about two little girls, Emily and Moonshine, and a beautiful wild goose. It is about their friendship and their adventures. It happened a long time ago, when television, computers and airplanes were not yet invented.

It was a lovely spring morning, when...

Emily rushed down to the lake to see whether the goose with the injured foot was feeling any better.

"It looks fine," she declared, examining the wound on the goose's foot, "I hope it won't happen again to any of you geese, walking around barefoot on the shore. My mom and I are going to put up a sign that says not to leave trash on the ground. Then nobody else will have to worry about stepping on rusty, old cans."

She carefully took the bandage off the webbed foot of the goose and said, "Well, now you are ready to swim and paddle!"

"Thank you Emily," honked the goose cheerfully. "I am really glad to be healthy in time to join the flock flying north for the summer. I am grateful that you helped me to get well! Please, tell me if there is anything I could do for you—do you have a wish I could help you to fulfill?"

"Oh thank you, gentle goose," said Emily. "I have so many wishes, it's hard to decide which one is the greatest. Let me think about it until tomorrow!"

The next day the goose was waiting for Emily at the willow tree.

"So, have you been thinking about your wish?" the goose asked.

"Yes," answered Emily, "What I would like to do the most is see my friend Moonshine. We have been writing to each other for a year now, but we have never met. She lives far away, you see, far up north. I wish I could fly like you geese, fly over the mountains, the rivers and the lakes and visit her in the land of the Inuit! But I can't."

"Yes you can! It's easy," said the goose. "Just jump on my back and we will fly north, we will fly until we reach them!"

"That would be wonderful," sighed Emily, "but am I too heavy for you to carry?"

"No, no, I am strong," said the goose proudly. "I am one of the few Giant Canada Geese! You can recognize us easily by the white mark on our forehead."

"And your mark is in the shape of a heart, because you are a good, kind goose!"

The day finally arrived. The big day when the geese were to begin their long journey to the north.

The younger geese were still playing in the lake when the elder of the flock, standing on the shore, loudly honked out the last call: "It's time to come out of the water! Dry your feathers and get ready!"

The older and wiser ones of the flock were busy preparing for the long flight, preening their wings, munching on rich, fresh grass.

Emily and the friendly goose were getting ready too. Emily did not say much, just silently buttoned the warm vest her mother had given her, along with a big hug, kisses and a few tears.

"Fasten your ribbons, Emily," said the goose. "We are lifting off."

Suddenly, the whole flock started honking wildly, ran a few yards on the ground, then all at the same time lifted up in the air, flapping their wings briskly.

The flock circled the lake once, as if saying good-bye, and then quickly arranging themselves into a neat V-formation, they flew off to the north.

Emily was breathless. She couldn't believe it—she was flying! Holding tight to the strong neck of the goose, she went higher and higher.

She didn't dare look back, or look down. She did not dare to move at all.

"Are you afraid?" asked the goose.

"No! No! I am not. It's just...it's just a bit unusual. I have never been this close to the sky before," said Emily.

"Do you miss your brothers and sisters?" asked the goose.

"I don't have any," said Emily, "but I miss my mom and dad. I'm an only child."

"Oh...and I was the only gosling," said the goose, "but I wish I had a sister."

"So do I," agreed Emily. "Hmm...do you mind if I call you Sister Goose?"

"That would be really nice, Emily," answered the goose, swiftly flapping her wings to catch up with the rest of the flock.

The geese were flying high above the hills and valleys, rivers and lakes, meadows and forests. They flew over wide fields and emerald marshlands, rocky mountains and deep canyons.

"Look, snow!" exclaimed Emily, when glistening white snow patches grew bigger and bigger on the rugged mountain peaks. "We will be there soon, don't you think, Sister Goose? I can hardly wait to see my friend Moonshine!"

"I am looking forward to seeing her too," said Sister Goose. "She has a beautiful name."

"Yes," agreed Emily. "When she was born, the full moon was shining all night and left thousands of little blue sparkles in her hair, so her mother called her Moonshine."

"There she is!" shouted Emily. "There they are! Moonshine and the kids! Do you see them, Sister Goose? They are waiting for us at the lake!"

"Yes, they are all there—the children from the village and that little girl must be Moonshine," said Sister Goose. "She's waving with bouquets of flowers!"

"Yes! Yes! They have noticed us! Please, Sister Goose, hurry!"

"I'll do my best, Emily," said Sister Goose. "Just a few more wing flaps and we will be landing on shore."

In a few minutes the whole flock of geese set down on the lake, honking cheerfully. They landed one after the other, stirring up the calm blue waters.

Sister Goose descended too with her passenger and swam to shore to let Emily off on the grassy banks so she could keep her boots dry.

Moonshine and the children quickly joined Emily and began singing a beautiful welcome song for Emily and Sister Goose. Moonshine gave Emily a big hug and a lovely wreath of pretty arctic flowers, such as lupine, cottongrass, poppy and saxifrage.

Everybody wanted to see the visitors from the south. While Sister Goose joined the flock for a swim, Moon-shine helped Emily to get acquainted with the birds and little furry friends of the Arctic meadows.

The northern sparrow and the handsome Arctic tern introduced themselves and the ptarmigan father excused his wife, who was busy taking care of the chicks.

Fluffy rabbits came to greet Emily and the curious little ermine was there too, of course.

The red squirrel and the tiny pika hurried to see Emily, and the ground squirrel, known as *sik-sik* by the Inuit kids also came out from its burrows.

The snowy owl was there too, but knowing that all of these small animals were terribly afraid of him, kept himself hidden among the branches of a nearby tree.

They all wanted to hear what Emily knew about their relatives living in the faraway southern forests and meadows, and she gladly answered all their questions.

The next day everybody went back to work. The birds were gathering food for their young, the rabbits nursed their babies and the bees continued to collect the sweet wildflower pollen to make their honey.

Moonshine's family kept busy too. Her father was repairing his kayak, getting it ready for the next hunting season. Little Bear, Moonshine's older brother helped his father attach a new seal skin cover to the kayak frame, while Quick Weasel, the youngest boy was unusually quiet watching them at work.

Moonshine's mother did not stop for a minute as she sewed the family's winter clothes, which were made of fur and leather. Humming a joyful tune, her fingers were stitching the heavy skins with remarkable ease.

"Children, would you like to take a trip down to the seashore?" asked Moonshine's father.

"Yes, yes, we are ready." answered Moonshine and the boys.

"Well, I ran out of walrus ivory for my carvings, and now I need a few tusks for making knife handles, tools and hair combs. The walruses should all be gone now for the summer, looking for cooler waters far up north. The rocky little islands are deserted now, so you could go and show Emily the place where those big animals like to gather by the hundreds, basking in the sun, sometimes fighting and wrestling, and very often breaking off their long tusks."

"I'm sure we will find some tusks among the rocks," said Little Bear.

Moonshine, Emily, Little Bear and Quick Weasel headed to the boat with their bags and baskets. They pushed the big family boat, called an *umiak*, into the water and jumped in. Little Bear and Moonshine took the paddles. Emily just sat admiring the lovely blooming meadows of the valley which followed the winding creek on its way to the sea. Quick Weasel couldn't sit still in the boat, of course, turning his head constantly so as not to miss any jumping trout in the water or soaring hawk high above.

But not even he noticed the herd of caribou, silently approaching on the high mossy banks, ready to cross the waters.

"Look," said the old bull with the magnificent antlers, "Emily is in the boat, the courageous girl from the south who flew here on the back of a goose to see her friend Moonshine."

The calm water of the little creek began to run faster and faster, hitting loudly against the stony banks, then rushing by the last big rocks, it suddenly pushed the boat into the ocean.

Little Bear knew exactly where to find the oogli, the walruses' favorite island and he turned the boat toward its rocky shore.

Quick Weasel saw the island and stood up in the boat shouting, "Forward! We are taking over the island of the beasts!"

"NO!" came the thundering reply from a walrus. A mountain of brown flesh with two bulging eyes and enormous white tusks, the walrus, emerging from the waves, put his huge flipper on the boat.

Quick Weasel lost his balance and with a big splash he fell into the chilly water. He scrambled back into the boat in a hurry.

The walrus was so mad, his whiskers were shaking as he ordered the children to leave. "The island is ours," he rumbled. "Three walrus families are staying here until the baby calves are strong enough to follow the herd to the icebergs."

"We are sorry to intrude," answered Little Bear politely, "but we are not hunters. We don't have any harpoons. All we want to do is gather thrown-away pieces of tusks." The walrus eyed them suspiciously. "Well...all right," said the walrus. "But do it fast."

The big walrus swam back to the island and let the children come ashore and quietly collect the broken pieces of tusk scattered around the rocks and in the crevices.

"Father is going to be so happy," said Little Bear as they filled the leather sacks with the precious tusks and loaded the *umiak*.

Paddling up stream was not as easy as gliding down, so when the boat was passing by a lush berry patch, Moonshine suggested they rest and pick some berries.

"Besides, Quick Weasel has to dry his clothes," she added.

They pulled up the boat, took out their baskets and the competition began: who could pick the most juicy yellow cloudberries?

Quick Weasel felt a little left out, sitting in the grass, wrapped in a blanket of caribou skin, watching his clothes dry in the sunshine.

"Mother makes wonderful jam with these berries," said Moonshine turning to Emily. "And we will help her!"

All of a sudden the children heard strange grunting noises from the other side of a nearby hill. They ran to see what it was.

There they were: large, scary-looking animals with big horns and long dark fur. It was a herd of musk-oxen standing still and closely together. In front of them on the open tundra stood two big bulls, staring and snorting at each other. Suddenly, they rushed forward, and there was a terrible bang as the bulls crashed their bony foreheads together.

The bulls backed off slowly, waited for a few seconds, growling nastily, then charged again, and again, until the weaker musk-ox got tired, turned around and ambled away.

The proud winner joined the herd and the musk-oxen continued quietly grazing on the lush green hillside. The children had never seen anything like it and were amazed at the size and power of the animals. They couldn't wait to get home to tell their parents about their exciting day. And Emily knew her parents would be thrilled to hear of her adventures.

While Emily, Moonshine and the boys were away on their boat trip, Sister Goose was peacefully walking around on the shore, enjoying the sunny afternoon, the buzz of the bees and the wonderful smell of fresh grass. Suddenly a shrill shriek cut through the air.

"This sound can only mean serious danger," Sister Goose said to herself and stretching out her long neck looked around. Right there under the bush stood the ptarmigan mother, shaking with fear.

"Please, Sister Goose, help," she pleaded. "The fox is stealing our children!"

"Stay right there," said Sister Goose quickly. "And you too," she said to father ptarmigan, who was about to rush to defend his chicks.

In a second Sister Goose was there at the nest, honking furiously at the fox, ready to attack the thief. The downy little ptarmigan chicks chirped desperately, trying to escape, while the three fox kits watched from behind the rocks. The fox, shocked by the threatening giant goose, took a step back then turned around and ran away, followed quickly by the little foxes.

27

The ptarmigan parents rushed to their babies and the happy family was united again.

Sister Goose was the hero of the day. Everybody was talking about her, the courageous lifesaver, who scared the nasty intruder away and saved the five little ptarmigans.

They decided to have a celebration in the flower fields. Everybody came: birds, big and small, the little

furry fellows from the valley and of course all the Inuit children with Moonshine and Emily.

They all joined in the happy song and dance on the blooming meadow.

Emily's thoughts wandered away to her distant home, to her mom and dad. She wished they could join her now on this day of joy, together with Moonshine, Sister Goose, the children, birds and animals, to celebrate their wonderful friendships.

It was time to get ready for the flight back home. Sister Goose didn't mind the extra baggage: the big jar of delicious cloudberry jam for Emily's mom, bone fishing hooks for Emily's dad, pretty combs of walrus ivory, and a beautiful little hood, edged with soft white fur of arctic fox—all gifts from Moonshine and her family.

Saying good-bye was not easy. Emily would miss the flowering hillside, the turquoise lake, the song and chatter of new friends, the birds and animals of the lovely Inuit land.

The hardest thing of all was saying good-bye to Moonshine, who was there with the other children, smiling with tears in her eyes, waving and saying, "Sister Goose and sweet Emily, farewell!"

The End.